Here Comes Tagalong

By Anne Mallett

Illustrated by Steven Kellogg

Parents' Magazine Press
New York

Text copyright © 1971 by Anne Mallett
Illustrations copyright © 1971 by Steven Kellogg
Printed in the United States of America
All rights reserved
ISBN: Trade 0-8193-0496-4, Library 0-8193-0497-2
Library of Congress Catalog Card Number: 78-153790

*

Here Comes Tagalong

Steve was five years old.

He had a father, a mother, a big brother and a little brother, and a new house to live in, in a new neighborhood.

When they first moved in, his mother allowed him
to go three houses from home on one side,
three houses from home on the other side,
but no farther.

"I always want to be able to see where
you are," she said.

There were lots of big boys close by,
but he never saw any little boys his size
in any of these houses. So he used
to tag along after his big brother and
his brother's friends.

They didn't mind because Steve was a good
kid and didn't get in their way.

But they didn't call him Steve.
They just called him Tagalong.

When they watched TV they let him watch, too.

When they played checkers, they let
him play one game.

Unfortunately he lost.

When they played ball, they put him in back
of the outfield and let him chase
the balls no one else was able to catch.

When it was his turn at bat, they decided
not to play ball any more.

They decided to build a tree house.

They let him hand the hammer and nails
and the boards up to them, but then he had
to stay on the ground and watch them. He was
too little to reach the first branch.

Later when they built a kite,
they let him run into the house
to get the paper.

"Watch out. You're tearing it!"
his brother yelled.

Steve got all tangled up in the string.

"That's not the way you make a tail,"
the big boys said scornfully.

When it was time to fly the kite, the boys
decided to take it to a big field three
blocks away where there was lots of room.
"You can't come," they said. "You're too little."

And they went off and left him all alone.

That was the day his mother told him he
could go all the way around the block if
he would promise not to cross the street.

When he got part way around the block,
he saw a little boy just his size.

Two houses farther on
there was another boy his size.

Four houses farther on, there were two more
little boys just his size.

They kept walking together, around the block,
until they came to Steve's house.

Steve showed them the tree house.
Some day soon they would be big enough
to climb up and play in it.

Then they had a ball game.
They all had a chance at bat and a
chance to pitch.

They made a kite.
Now he knew the right way to make a tail.
And when he got a little tangled up
in the string, his friends didn't care.

There was a nice wind blowing.

When they went into the house they played
checkers, and Steve won one of the games.

When they all sat down and watched TV,
they let Steve's little brother watch with them
because he was a good kid and didn't get
in their way.

After that, Steve's little brother had a new name.
Whenever they saw him, Steve and his friends said,

"Here comes Tagalong!"

Anne Mallett is also the author of *Whopper Whale,* which she illustrated, and *Who'll Mind Henry?* a Junior Literary Guild selection. In addition to writing and painting, she loves gardening, cooking, sewing, and climbing "small" mountains; and she has also worked as a draftsman, designed textiles, and taught in the Worcester Art Museum School.

Mrs. Mallett was born in Worcester, Massachusetts, and attended the Boston Museum School of Fine Arts and the Fontainebleau School in France. She and her husband, an art director, live in Natick, Massachusetts, and have two children who are in college.

A graduate of the Rhode Island School of Design in Providence, *Steven Kellogg* had a year's study in Italy, taught etching at American University in Washington, D.C., and has had his etchings and drawings exhibited in Washington and New York.

Mr. Kellogg has illustrated, among others, *Martha Matilda O'Toole, The Rotten Book, Gwot!* and *Brave Johnny O'Hare,* the latter by Eleanor B. Heady, published by Parents'.

Mr. Kellogg and his wife, Helen, and their six children live in Sandy Hook, Connecticut.